SARAI
AND THE MEANING OF AWESOME

SARAI GONZALEZ
AND
MONICA BROWN

SCHOLASTIC INC.

Text copyright © 2018 by Sarai Gonzalez
Illustrations by Christine Almeda copyright © 2018 by Scholastic Inc.

ISBN 978-1-338-23668-2

10 9 8 7 6 5 4 3 2 1   18 19 20 21 22

Printed in the U.S.A.   40
First printing 2018

Book design by Carolyn Bull

To Tata, Mama Rosi, and my very special third-grade
teacher, Mrs. Pirrone.
-SG

This book is dedicated to ALL girls—
funny, fierce, and unique! You can change the world.
-MB

CONTENTS

INTRODUCTION: I, SARAI 2

CHAPTER 1: TATA'S TROUBLES 12

CHAPTER 2: CUPCAKE POWER 22

CHAPTER 3: SNAP! 28

CHAPTER 4: THE BIG BAKE 38

CHAPTER 5: FLYING 50

CHAPTER 6: BIG PLANS 58

CHAPTER 7: LIMONADA AND CHICHA MORADA 72

CHAPTER 8: ¡FIESTA! 82

CHAPTER 9: THE SUPER AWESOME SISTER FUN CLUB 92

CHAPTER 10: THE MEANING OF AWESOME 100

I, SARAI

I wake up in the morning, open my eyes, and stare at the painted sign hanging above my bed. It says "YOU ARE AWESOME." I made it to remind myself that no matter what else is going on, I'll be okay. Because I, Sarai Gonzalez, am awesome. Or, at least I try to be. My sister Lucía once asked me what awesome means, and it was a little hard to explain. Awesome means, well, awesome! It also means great, super, amazing, and love, family, and fun. It's how I want to be and what I hope I already am.

One day, I want to be a singer, a dancer, an actor, a baker, a talk show host, and a chef. I already AM a businesswoman, or business girl, I guess, since I'm only ten. I have a cupcake business, and my pink-and-yellow room is the same color as the strawberry-lemon cupcakes I made last week for my mom's friend. I used boxed mixes for the cake part, but I made homemade frosting and decorated them with sprinkles and a cherry on top. I take cupcake making seriously, because it's a business. I even have cards that say "Sarai's Sweets" with my dad's number on them. I only sell to people I know. I'm always trying to earn money because it seems like someone in the family always needs it, and I want to be able to help. For a long time we needed help with our bills and we moved from place to place. We are doing great now, but I remember how much our family helped us when we needed it, so I have two coffee cans where I save my money. One says "Family" and the other says "Bike" because I'm also saving up to buy a bike. I want my bike to be hot pink, my favorite color, and have ribbons and stickers and a really loud horn.

When I ride my super awesome bike down the street, I want the neighbors to say, "Here comes Sarai Gonzalez!" as I fly by in a pink blur.

Being a member of the Gonzalez family means a lot. The Gonzalez family five is my mom, my dad, my little sister Josie, and my little sister Lucía. Josie is seven, and Lucía is five. And me, of course. My mom still calls me her "little peanut," but I'm not so little anymore. I'm in the fourth grade! We stick together, no matter what. When we go to a party or church or anywhere, people make room.

"Here comes the Gonzalez family!" they say. "Look out!" At first, I didn't know what that meant, but Dad says it means that we are *very* fun and loud.

My mom, Diana, was born in Peru, all the way in South America. She moved here when she was a little girl with her mother and sister and she worked in the farm fields when she was only fourteen. My mom is hardworking, and I want to be just like her. Even though her family didn't have a lot of money, she went to college and now she works with computers.

My mom says we can be anything we want when we grow up, and I believe her.

My dad, Juan Carlos, is an immigrant too. He came to the United States when he was little, and just like my mom, he was the first in his family to go to college. Dad is from Costa Rica, in Central America, but our whole family lives in New Jersey now. So we are really, truly Americans—North, South, and Central!

A few years ago, my parents bought us our very first house. It's small and white and has three bedrooms. Before we bought the house, we lived in apartments or with other people—grandparents, cousins, aunts and uncles. That was fun, but it's pretty cool to have my very own room for the first time. I've got purple flowers painted on the door, and I'm growing flowers and vegetables on my windowsill—sunflowers and cabbage and peas and broccoli. When they get bigger, Dad will help me plant them outside. Dad and I love doing projects together. My dad is an at-home dad, which is kind of a silly thing to say, because my mom is at home a lot too, just not during weekdays.

During the weekdays, the Gonzalez family five have to spend some time apart. Lucía and I go to school together, Mom goes to work, and Dad drives Josie very far away to a different school. Josie is hearing impaired and goes to a school with other deaf and hearing-impaired children. She just got implants in her ears that help her hear sounds— it's pretty awesome! She's also learning sign language, and we're trying too. Josie has already learned lots of words, like "pool," "ice cream," and the name of her favorite hamburger place, for starters. She can sign my name too.

Most people pronounce my name SAR-EYE. I like it. My grandparents on both sides pronounce my name the Spanish way—SAH-RAH-EEE. It's kind of funny because in English, Sarai (SAR-EYE) rhymes with *"I,"* and in Spanish, Sarai (SAH-RAH-EEE) rhymes with *"me!"* I, Sarai, think that's pretty awesome.

CHAPTER 1

TATA'S TROUBLES

When the school bus drops Lucía and me off in front of our house on Carmen Street, our Tata is waiting on the porch. We're really lucky because he comes over to watch us every day after school. Today, he's listening to music on an old radio and talking to his cell phone in Spanish.

"¿Cómo estás, Siri?" Tata asks the phone.

"Lo siento como pez en el agua," the phone answers back. Who ever heard of a phone feeling like a fish in the water? Tata showed me how he changed

the phone settings to Spanish. It turns out Siri knows
lots of languages and has a sense of humor.

"Tata!" I say. "Ever since you got a smartphone,
you never get off of it!"

He looks up and smiles. My Tata loves gadgets.
He just retired from being an electrician. When he
was young, he worked as a helicopter mechanic in the
navy. Tata is always fiddling with radios and cameras
and fans and anything he can get his hands on. He
has lots of old phones and radios and appliances.
He especially loves his phone.

"¡Hola, nietas!" Tata says. "How are my beautiful granddaughters? Come inside. We'll listen to music while I heat you up some food." Another song comes on—"The Twist." It's one of Tata's favorites.

"This song is by Chubby Checker!" Tata says, standing up and showing us how to do this crazy dance move called the twist. We try to move and shake like him, but end up just breaking out in laughter.

Tata loves to dance just as much as we do.

"Tata! Watch me!" Lucía says, twisting from left to right.

"I've got a new move," I say, and spin my head so that my braids fly around like a pinwheel.

Finally, Tata says, "You girls have tired me out. Who's hungry?"

When Tata babysits, he always brings us Peruvian food from my grandma Mama Rosi. It's the best.

"I am! What did Mama Rosi make us today?" I ask.

"Chaufa!" he says.

"Yay!" I say. That's one of my favorites. Chaufa sounds like CHOW-FA in English, and it is yummy Peruvian-Chinese fried rice. It has onions, vegetables, soy sauce, oil, and little pieces of cut-up hot dogs. Tata brings us enough food to have leftovers. Mama Rosi is teaching me how to make

Peruvian food too. Someday I want to go to Peru and visit the place where my mom and family were born. I'm happy because a lot of my family lives here now, including my aunt and uncle who I call Tía and Tío. They have three kids. We call them the Js, because all my cousins' names start with J: JuJu, which is short for Juliana, and the twins, Javier and Jade.

♡JUJU♡ ♡

✯Javier✯

✿Jade✿

The Js live with Tata and Mama Rosi in their big house. I think everyone in our family has lived with Tata and Mama Rosi at one point or another. JuJu is my exact age and she's my super best cousin-friend. We don't go to the same school, but we see each other almost every weekend.

Today, while Lucía and I are eating our chaufa, Tata gets a call and steps out onto the porch to talk. He's out there a long time, and by the time he comes back, we are done eating and Tata is frowning. My Tata never frowns, not even when we make a mess or argue or break one of his gadgets.

"Tata!" I say. "What's going on?"

"Nothing," he says, and the phone rings again. He goes outside for a long time, and when he comes back, I say, "I know something's wrong. What is it?"

"Just a little bit of bad news," he says.

"What kind of bad news?" I shout, jumping up from the table. I don't like bad news.

"Well, I was hoping this wouldn't happen, but it finally has. It looks like we are going to have to move. The owner of the house we've been renting for almost twenty years is going to sell it, and I don't think we can afford to buy it."

"Move?" I ask. "You can't! That's *your* house, and you've been there forever!" I say. I love Tata and Mama Rosi's house. When Josie was having health problems, or whenever we were short on money, we could always move back into my grandparents' house for a little bit. It seems like my home too. And it's filled with the people I love.

"What will happen to the Js?" I ask. "And Tía Sofía and Tío Miguel? And you and Mama Rosi? Where will you go? What if we never see each other again? This is a disaster!" I start crying, and Lucía does too.

"I don't want you to go away," Lucía says. "I want the family to be together."

"It's not a disaster," Tata says, trying to smile and not doing a very good job. "There are much worse things that can happen, Sarai. We will find a new home."

"Will it be far away?" Lucía asks.

"I hope not," Tata says.

"Promise you won't move far away, Tata," I tell him.

"Sarai," he says. "It's too soon to make promises. I need to talk to Mama Rosi and your parents. For now, don't worry." Tata goes into the kitchen, looking for something. "Enough of this sad talk—Mama Rosi also made some alfajores! Let's have something sweet to get rid of these sad tears."

"Yum!" Lucía says, reaching for an alfajores. They are my favorite. Two round, crumbly butter cookies with caramel in the middle and powdered sugar on top. I take one too. Lucía opens hers up and licks the caramel.

"Barriga llena, corazón contento," Tata says. "Full stomach, happy heart." That's one of his favorite sayings. But how can I have a happy heart when Tata and Mama Rosi are going to have to move?

CHAPTER 2

CUPCAKE POWER

When my mom gets home from work, I'm feeling really anxious. She and Tata talk for a long time in Spanish. As soon as he leaves, I turn to my mom. "I want to help Tata and Mama Rosi keep their house," I say. "I don't want them to move! That's so unfair. Can't we buy the house for them?"

"Slow down, Sarai," Mom says. "Take a deep breath. It isn't possible for us to buy the house."

"Nothing is impossible," I say back.

"You are sweet, little peanut," she says. "But with Tata retired, the house is too expensive."

"We can't give up!" I say, and Mom comes over and gives me a hug.

Apparently, Lucía isn't as worried as I am, because she says, "I know how we can cheer everyone up. We can go to Hawaii this weekend!" Lucía is obsessed with Hawaii, and none of us are exactly sure why. She always talks about the islands and the ocean and the sand and really seems to think that one morning we are going to get in the van and drive there.

"Not this weekend," Mom says, smiling, and just then Dad and Josie walk through the door.

"I'm too tired to cook," Dad says.

"Me too," Mom says. "Let's go out to eat!"

"But we need to do something about Tata and Mama Rosi's house!" I say, and we fill in Dad and Josie.

"We'll talk more over dinner," Mom says. "Where should we go?"

"I want a panini," I say.

"Hamburgers!" Josie shouts.

"Chicken!" says Lucía.

As usual, we all want different things.

"Okay, kids," Dad says. "Let's get into the rectangle." We call our minivan the rectangle because it looks like one.

"Yay! All five?" Josie asks, holding up five fingers. That's Josie's way of asking if we're going to go somewhere all together.

"All five!" says Dad, smiling. Then Dad drives us to three different restaurants so we can each take out what we want. By then, we are all so hungry that we don't wait until we get home. We just park our car behind the last place, and we eat, laugh, talk, and listen to music in our rectangle.

I feel good, surrounded by my family. And even better, I have an idea—an idea to help save Tata and Mama Rosi's house.

"I know!" I say. "I'm a business girl. I can work and make enough money to buy Tata and Mama Rosi's house for them!"

"Houses are very expensive," Mom says.

"What if I make Sarai's Sweets a bigger business? I've never had an unsatisfied customer!"

"I can help!" says Lucía.

"Me too," Josie signs and says.

"Super awesome sister power!" I shout.

Mom and Dad look concerned.

"We can do this!" I say. "I know we can."

CHAPTER 3

SNAP!

When we come home from school the next day, Tata isn't waiting on the porch. We find him at the kitchen table, fiddling with an old typewriter. It has a cord and it's plugged in and it's humming, almost buzzing.

"What's this?" Lucía asks, smoothing her fingers over the keys.

"It's what we used before we had computers," Tata says. "It's an electric typewriter, and I just fixed it."

She touches one of the keys, and there's a loud snap. Lucía snatches her hand back. The machine hums.

"I want to try!" I say, and I hit one key after another. *Snap! Snap! Snap! Snap! Snap!*

"It sounds alive," Lucía says, making Tata and I laugh.

"Let's put some paper in," says Tata, "and we can test it out. I just changed the ink." Tata sets me up, and I sit down and type a sentence.

My name is Sarai Gonzalez and I am awesome.

Sarai's Sweets = cupcake power

I love the sound of the typewriter keys banging on the paper, and I love the blue ink.

This is so cool!!!!!!!!!!!!!!!!!!!!!!!

I have an idea and keep typing.

Tata, will you come with Lucía and I to take some cupcake orders for Sarai's Sweets?

Please??????????

Pretty please???????

Por favor?????????

"Stop!" says Lucía, covering her ears. "It's too loud. And that noise sounds like insects buzzing. Yuck!"

I pull out the sheet, and I hand it to Tata.

"Of course, I'll walk with you to take cupcake orders," Tata says. "Lucía, do you want a turn at typing first?"

"No," she says, "I definitely don't."

"Tata," I say, "do you know why I want to sell a lot of cupcakes?"

"Why, Sarai?" he asks. "Is it to buy a new bike?"

"No," I say. "It's so we can buy your house so you don't have to move."

"¡Nieta!" he says. "You don't need to worry about us—at all. We will figure things out. No more of this talk. You use your money for a new bicycle."

"But we want to help," says Lucía. "And Josie does too!"

"The world better watch out for my grand-daughters, because they don't take no for an answer," Tata says, shaking his head. Then we go to collect cupcake orders.

Tata walks us from house to house and waits while we walk up to the door and knock.

"¡Hola, Señora Sanchez!" I say. Señora Sanchez is even older that Tata, I think, and she has thick gray hair that she wraps around the top of her head in a huge bun. I know she likes sweets, because she always offers them to us when she's out in her yard. She's out there a lot, and she has the prettiest flowers on the street. I tell her all about my cupcakes and our plan to save Tata and Mama Rosi's house. "Sarai's Sweets is open for business!" I tell her.

"Sarai and her sisters," Lucía corrects me. Señora Sanchez puts in an order for a dozen strawberry-lemon cupcakes.

"You don't pay until delivery," I tell her as I wave goodbye over my shoulder.

"¡Suerte!" she says. "Good luck!"

Next, we visit the Washington family. Mr. and Mrs. Washington have four boys! They order two dozen s'mores cupcakes, and the Garcias, a retired couple that live next door, order a dozen more. Mr. Garcia knows Tata from church, so he comes out and they talk for a while about old cars, old songs, and fútbol—which is called soccer here in the US.

By the time we finish walking around the block, my order sheet is almost full.

"Look!" I show Mom and Dad when they get home. I've got orders for a dozen strawberry-lemon cupcakes, two dozen s'mores cupcakes, a dozen cookies-and-cream cupcakes, and one Cupcake Surprise—that's Tata's order, which he insisted on paying us for. Since it's all going toward buying his house, I said okay.

SARAI'S SWEETS

ORDERS

strawberry-lemon ×12

s'mores ×24

cookies & cream ×12

"I have a couple more orders from work," Mom says. "It's going to be a busy Saturday. I hope you are all ready to work."

"Of course we are," I say.

"I want to decorate!" says Lucía.

"Sister power!" Josie says and signs.

"Are we going to shop tonight?" asks Lucía.

"Please, Dad?" I say, even though he looks a little tired.

"Okay, Sarai," Dad says with his usual smile, and grabs the keys to the rectangle.

By the time we go to the store, unload baking supplies, and get ready for bed, I'm exhausted. I make sure to set my alarm so I don't sleep in too late. Tomorrow is a big day! I fall asleep almost as soon as my head hits the pillow, and I dream I'm walking in a magic forest toward a house made of strawberry cupcakes.

WOW!

CHAPTER 4

THE BIG BAKE

My alarm goes off on Saturday morning, and I hop out of bed and start organizing the kitchen.

"It's not even seven yet, Sarai," Dad says, coming out of his room in his robe, "and it's a Saturday."

"It's my favorite day! I want it to be long," I say. "Besides, Tata always says that the early bird gets the worm."

"The early bird can have the worm," jokes Dad. "I want coffee."

Mom gets up soon after, and then the girls wake

up too. Mom and Dad make us a yummy breakfast,
and when we are done, I say, "Josie, Lucía, it's time!
Are you ready to bake?"

"Yes!" Josie signs and says.

"Definitely!" Lucía says, and then Mom makes us
wash our hands with soap and water.

"First," I say, "we need to make the batter." It's
not going to be too hard, because I use boxes—
we've got chocolate batter, vanilla batter, lemon
batter, and strawberry batter. I figure out the different
proportions, and pretty soon, we all have a job. Lucía

and Josie are opening the boxes, Dad is cutting the
bags, and I'm pouring the powder into different
bowls. Next it's time to add the eggs and oil.

"I want to crack the eggs!" Lucía says.

"Me too!" Josie signs and says. I teach my sisters
how to crack the egg gently on the side of the bowl. I
guess they like the sound of eggs cracking
because—SPLAT!

Both Lucía and Josie hit the eggs on the bowl
too hard, and the eggs splatter onto the counter.

"Gentle!" I say. They try again and again but can't
seem to get it. The raw eggs have started dripping
down the counter and onto the floor.

"Great," I say. "Now there's gross yellow goo
everywhere."

"It's sticky!" Josie signs and says. Then she runs a
finger through the mess.

"Watch!" says Lucía. "I bet I'll stick to the floor."

Then she puts her foot into the mess on the floor to test her theory. Josie picks up another egg.

"Stop!" I say, and make Lucía take off her shoes. I take the egg from Josie and crack the rest of the eggs myself.

"What's next?" Lucía asks.

"I have to pick the shells out of the batter," I say grumpily. Then, I pour in the oil and let my sisters take turns mixing. Josie and Lucía mix so fast that some of the batter splatters, but not too much.

"I thought we'd go faster with everyone working," I tell Mom as I try to clean up after my sisters. "Clearly I was wrong!" The kitchen counter is a disaster.

"Sarai, let's not bother cleaning until the end," Mom suggests.

"Good idea," I say, and then I turn to my sisters. "We need to decide what we want as our Cupcake Surprise flavor, so start brainstorming."

"Chocolate!" Josie signs and says.

"Banana!" Lucía says.

"Those flavors aren't very surprising," I say, frowning. "But if we mix banana into the vanilla batter and make chocolate frosting, that might be pretty cool."

"Yay!" the girls say. They are so excited they start jumping up and down, which is fine, except Lucía trips and knocks over one of the bowls of strawberry batter. It splatters all over my pink-and-purple polka-dot pants. Luckily we still have another bowl left.

"Argh!" I say. "I guess our strawberry-lemon cupcakes will be more lemon than strawberry."

Dad walks in and sees the chaos. "Girls," Dad says to Lucía and Josie, "why don't you take a break and we'll walk to the park while Mom and Sarai fill up the cupcake tins and get them cooking?"

"Yes," I say with a huff, "why don't you?" Mom and I get busy filling the cups and getting them in the oven. By the time Dad and the girls come back from the park, we have only one bowl of batter left to bake.

Dad walks through the door with Lucía and Josie when—

"AAAAHH!" Josie screams, and points toward Lucía.

"What?" Lucía asks.

"There's a cricket in your hair!" I say, reaching toward her head to flick it off.

"Ahhhhhhhh!" Lucía cries, swatting at her hair. The cricket goes flying . . . right into the vanilla batter.

"Oh no!" I say. "It's ruined."

"Just mix it in extra good," Dad says, joking. "Isn't that batch supposed to be a Cupcake Surprise?"

"No way," Mom says, shaking her head at Dad.

"Now we need to go to the store *again*," I say to my sisters, "and it's all your fault!"

JOOSH! UH-OH

"No, it isn't!" Josie signs and says.

"You're using a mean voice!" Lucía says loudly.

"Well, so are you!" I shout.

"It was an accident," Dad reminds me, but it doesn't make me any less upset. We sit down to lunch, and afterward, Dad runs me to the grocery store, where I buy more ingredients. Baking is costing more than I thought.

When we get back, we start decorating the rest of the cupcakes, which are cooled and ready. The girls decorate the cookies-and-cream cupcakes, but they keep eating the frosting. I tell them they have to stop or we won't have enough for the orders. They don't like this at all, so they quit. With a little help from Mom and Dad, I finish the rest of the orders and finally—it seems like hours later—we are done!

"Cleanup time!" I tell my sisters, but they aren't interested. "What happened to super awesome sister power? Get up and help!"

"It's not your job to tell us what to do!" Lucía says, and I guess Josie agrees, because they go into their room and shut the door with a loud bang.

I start cleaning. Why does it seem like I have to do *everything* by myself?

CHAPTER 5

FLYING

The next day is Sunday, and we all get into the rectangle to go to church. We always get to church early because Mom and Dad are in the choir. Everyone in my family loves to sing. Tata and Mama Rosi are also in the choir, and if I catch Tata's eye, he winks at me. During mass, I'm supposed to be in charge of my sisters, which doesn't always work out perfectly—like today, for example. The service has just started when Josie and Lucía start arguing over something and pushing each other in the pews.

"No fighting in church!" I whisper as loud as I can, but the trouble is they are not whispering—they are talking loud, so they don't even hear me. Or maybe they don't want to hear me. It seems like they're still upset from yesterday's argument. I get up and move to sit between them, and somehow, someone, accidentally or not, elbows me in the ribs.

"Ouch!" I say, and it isn't in a whisper. My Tía Sofía, who is in the row ahead of me, looks back at me with a question mark in her eyes.

Baby ME!

"Shhh!" she tells the girls, and I try not to get frustrated. I'm feeling wiggly too, but I need to be a good example, because they are only five and seven, and everyone tells me that I used to be the exact same way. When I was a toddler, I used to knock things down a lot. It was my favorite game, which was fine with blocks, but not so fine with plates and glasses full of water. I close my eyes and try not to listen to the mumbling and grumbling on either side of me. I'm so distracted with so many things running through my head.

What if my family moves far away? Will they have to go to another church? I tell myself, *I will fix this.* And then I think of all the things I have to do to help buy back the house. Because we had to buy more eggs and cake mix for the cupcakes, we only made a little money and I want my "Family" coffee can to be filled to the brim. I have to see if I can get more cupcake orders. I have to think of another idea. I have to . . .

And then, just as I'm adding one more "to do" to my to-do list, the organ starts to play and the choir starts to sing. I finally start to feel peaceful.

After church, my parents drive us straight to the park because, as Dad says, "You obviously have extra energy you want to get out."

"Now you can run and jump and be as loud as you want," Mom says, and she sits on a bench under the oak tree. Josie and Lucía run to the monkey bars, and Dad drives off to get us lunch. When he gets back, we'll have a picnic. I go straight to the swings. My favorite. I swing and I swing and I pump my legs higher and higher until I can almost touch the sky. It's so blue and pretty. I feel happy. Then, when I'm swinging as high as I can, I let go and jump off. For a second, it feels like I'm flying. I'm always a little disappointed when my feet hit the ground.

CHAPTER 6

BIG PLANS

On Monday morning, I wake up and the sun is shining through my window, and I notice that my cabbage plant is finally sprouting. I look at the "YOU ARE AWESOME" sign above my bed, and I feel good again, like I can do anything. I have a new idea, one that doesn't involve eggs or batter or little sisters who are afraid of crickets. My new plan to save Tata and Mama Rosi's house needs some cousin power, so I call my cousin JuJu.

"How's it going?" I ask her.

"Not so good," JuJu says. "I don't want to switch schools, and Mama Rosi has cried twice this week! Worst of all, there's a sign in front of our house saying 'For Sale' with big letters. There's a picture of a lady smiling. It says, "Call Molly Smith for more information.' I don't know what she's so happy about!"

"Who is Molly Smith, and why does she get to sell your house?" I say.

"She's the real estate agent," JuJu explains.

"Well, go outside right now and copy down her number so I can call her if we need to negotiate."

"You can't do that! We'll get in trouble," says JuJu. "We're not allowed to talk to strangers."

"How's she a stranger if her face is on your front lawn?" I ask. "Just get me her number. And don't worry. We have bigger problems. We need to figure out how we are going to buy the house. We have to do something," I say. "And I mean DO with capital letters."

"We need to make some money," JuJu says, "and fast!" I agree.

"Come over after school today and bring your best ideas!" I tell her.

"I will!" she says, and hangs up.

Later that day, the bus drops Lucía and me off, and JuJu is already on the porch. I grab her arm.

"Cousin conference! Right now, in my room." Lucía wants to come, but Tata understands that I need some older-kid time, so he invites Lucía to walk over to the bodega to get a paleta. Lucía loves Popsicles, so she agrees without too much fuss.

JuJu and I flop on my bed and she says, "Okay, you first. What's your idea?"

"Here's my plan," I say. "Why don't we have a lemonade stand over here Saturday afternoon?"

"That's a great idea!" JuJu says.

"All we need is lemons, sugar, water, and paper cups," I say. "You can come over as early as you can on Saturday, and bring all the pitchers you have. Also bring any change you can find around the house. Look in the sofa if you have to!"

"We'll need to make signs and flyers," JuJu says.

"And lemonade!" I say.

"Limonada," JuJu says. "We'll make the signs in English and Spanish."

"Wait!" I say. "I just thought of something that rhymes with limonada—chicha morada!"

Chicha morada is a special drink made out of purple corn from Peru. I love it, and I bet our neighbors will too.

"That would be awesome!" JuJu says. "I'll bring spices, and we'll buy the rest. Where will we get the purple corn?"

"They sell it at Mr. Martínez's bodega by our house. My mom buys it for special occasions."

"Well, this sure is a special occasion—we are going to save our house!" JuJu says.

"Okay, it's a plan," I tell JuJu. "Now tell me *your* idea."

"If you think you are ready for something AMAZING, I will," JuJu says.

"Totally," I say.

"Well, first, I have a question. Who are the best dancers that you know?" JuJu asks.

"That's easy," I say, smiling. "Us!"

"Well . . . look what I found," JuJu says, and hands me a piece of paper. It says "Garden State Kids Dance-Off: Audition Guidelines," and before I can even read the small print, JuJu snatches it back and says, "This is our big chance, Sarai! We just need to put together a two-minute dance video and submit it online with our parents' permission form. The winners get one thousand dollars and an agent!"

"Wow!" I say. "That's so much money! Let's do it!"

"Yes!" says JuJu. "But we don't have a lot of time because the video auditions are due by Friday!"

"Friday! That's only four days away."

"Yes, but my mom said she'd pick me up after school and bring me to your house every day this week, and Tata doesn't mind bringing me home after."

"Well," I say, pretending I have to think about it. "We haven't practiced dancing since the summer, and it could be really hard . . ."

"Since when are we afraid of hard?" JuJu asks, putting her hands on her hips.

"Since . . . NEVER!" I say, laughing. "What will we call ourselves?"

"The Sparkling Superstars?" JuJu says.

"The Dancing Divas?" I say back.

"We're dancers, not divas," JuJu says.

"That's true, Prima," I say. Then I have it. Prima means cousin in Spanish.

"How about the Playful Primas?" I say.

"Yes!" JuJu says. "That's perfect." Just then, we hear Tata and Lucía come back in the house, and Lucía bursts into the room.

"We got you some paletas!" Lucía says.

"Thanks! We're going to need all the energy we can get," I say, grabbing a paleta. We walk into the family room and tell them about our big plans.

"Will you help me with videotaping and music, Tata?" I say.

"Of course, mis reinas," he says, calling us his queens.

"I want to be in the Playful Primas too!" says Lucía. I'm about to say no way, but JuJu jumps in.

"You have to be at least eight to participate, LuLu. I'm sorry, but you can dance with us until we're ready to video."

I wait for Lucía to get mad, but she doesn't. I think maybe JuJu uses a nicer voice than me.

"First, we need to choose a song," I say. "Any ideas?"

"Beyoncé!" JuJu says.

"Marc Anthony," I say.

"Selena!" Lucía says. And then she sings, "Bidi bidi bom bom," the lyrics from her favorite song.

"Wow!" says JuJu. "That's the original Selena."

"She likes Selena Gomez too," I say, smiling. "How about salsa music?"

"I can help you with that!" Tata says. "And I think I have the perfect song for you, and it's perfect because it's sung by a queen! Celia Cruz, the Queen of Salsa, la reina de la salsa." He gets out his phone and plays a song.

"La vida es un carnaval," Celia sings, which means life is like a carnival. It's an awesome song.

"This song is perfect," JuJu says. "Celia is saying that life is beautiful, no matter what."

"And that you must live it singing!" Tata says.

"And dancing!" I say. "Let's start planning our dance!" We have so much fun practicing moves. I do the sprinkler, and JuJu spins and lands in a split. Tata teaches us some authentic salsa moves, and we are full of ideas.

The rest of the week goes fun and fast. We practice every day after school, and on Friday afternoon, we are finally ready to record. Tata sets up the camera and gives Lucía a flashlight to shine above us like a spotlight. We don't have time for super-fancy costumes, but we each wear bright pink shirts and overall shorts. They are nice and loose to dance in, and we braid our long black hair with colorful ribbons and borrow Mom's lipstick to put matching pink hearts on our cheeks. This is it.

"Action!" Tata says, starting the song. We dance as hard as we can, and when we finish we say, "We are the Playful Primas, and life is a carnival!" Then we take a bow.

"Cut!" Tata says, and that's it. We're done. Tata and Lucía clap, and then Tata helps us upload and turn in the video to the Garden State Kids Dance-Off. We are tired but happy. And hopeful.

CHAPTER 7

LIMONADA AND CHICHA MORADA

On Saturday morning, the doorbell rings early. It's the Js. All of them! Tía Sofía has brought everyone over, and we barely all fit in our house.

"Hola, Sarai," Tía Sofía says, giving me a great big hug. "We've been telling our friends to stop by this afternoon. This is a great idea!"

"When life gives you lemons, the Gonzalez family makes limonada!" Dad says, and everyone laughs. All the other kids go outside to play, and JuJu and I get to work.

Together we have almost fifteen dollars, and we look underneath furniture and in jacket pockets until we have a little more than seventeen dollars. We ask our parents if we can go to the corner market to buy supplies.

"Ice is heavy," says Dad. "I'll come to help you carry it."

"We'll take the wagon!" I say. "We can do it." We walk out the door, and we are nearly hit by Josie racing around in her toy car. The twins, Javier and Jade, are chasing her screaming, "We're gonna get you!"

The twins are six, a year younger than Josie and a year older than Lucía.

"We are not a quiet family," JuJu says.

"We sure aren't," I agree, smiling.

We walk the three blocks to the store, pulling the wagon behind us, and it's such a nice day, it seems like everyone in the neighborhood is outside. Kids are running through the sprinklers and playing tag, and the adults are working in their gardens or sitting on their porches or washing their cars. They wave, and I wave back. I invite the neighbors to come over to visit our lemonade stand later and explain that we're trying to save my grandparents' house. They are especially excited when I tell them we will have homemade chicha morada.

"This is a perfect day for a cool drink," I tell JuJu.

"Definitely," she agrees, and we walk into the bodega. It's called Martínez and Sons, but I've never seen anybody but Mr. Martínez behind the counter. Someone told me his sons grew up and moved away.

"Hello, Mr. Martínez!" I say. "How are you?"

"Muy bien, Sarai," he says, answering me in Spanish. JuJu gets a big bag of ice out of the freezer in the back of the store, and Mr. Martínez carries it out to the wagon. I get a bag of lemons, sugar, dried purple corn, a pineapple, and paper cups. The total comes to $18.01 and we only have $17.45!

"Let's make a deal," I tell Mr. Martínez, and explain what we are doing and why. "If you help us out, you can have a free glass of lemonade or chicha morada, and we are charging one dollar a glass, so you'll come out ahead."

"Hmmmmm," says Mr. Martínez, but I can tell he's only pretending to think about it.

"I'll bring you a cupcake next time I make them . . ." I say.

"Deal!" he says, smiling, and off we go.

SUGAR

With Mom's help, we place the purple corn into a big pot of water and add some cloves, sugar, lemon juice, and a few cinnamon sticks. Then we put it on the stove to boil. Mom cuts up the pineapple and JuJu and I squeeze lemons until our fingers are tingling. We mix the lemons and water and sugar, trying to get it just right.

"More sugar," I tell JuJu after a taste.

"More?" JuJu asks.

"Yes! We want everyone who drinks our lemonade to have a sweet day," I say. Pretty soon we have five pitchers of lemonade.

The chicha morada is almost done, and our whole house smells delicious. Now it's time for the sign! We make one giant sign that reads,

Delicious Lemonade/Limonada!
$1 for a (big) glass!
(That's ONLY four quarters!)
Delicious Purple-corn-ade/Chicha Morada

Then we use Tata's typewriter to make some smaller signs for our street corners.

```
Lemonade/Limonada/Chicha Morada!

       THE GONZALEZ HOUSE

       LA CASA GONZALEZ

     Come now! ¡Ven ahora!
```

Mom helps us strain the chicha morada, and soon we have pitchers of bright purple juice over ice. JuJu and I set up the table outside on the driveway with our colorful drinks. Dad helps by driving us around the neighborhood to put up our signs. We ask Lucía, Josie, and the twins to help us advertise, and they decide that means running up and down the street yelling, "Lemonade! Limonada! Chicha morada! At the Gonzalez house! Only one dollar a glass!"

"Come now while supplies last!"

"Come to our driveway and bring money!"

"Lots of money!"

I can't tell who is yelling what, but I can hear my sisters and cousins all the way down the street. We're the Gonzalez family, and we are loud. And open for business.

DELICIOUS LEMONAD
$1 for a (big) glass
(That's ONLY four quarter
Delicious Purple-corn

CHAPTER 8

¡FIESTA!

Pretty soon it seems like we have the whole neighborhood in our front yard. I'm so excited when my dad's parents, my other grandparents, surprise us by showing up! They live a little farther away than Tata and Mama Rosi and the Js, so I don't see them as often.

"Hi, Papá! Hi, Mama Chila!" I say. "Yay!" I leave the stand to run over and give them a giant hug. "How did you know to come?"

"A little bird told us," Mama Chila says. The little

bird must have been busy, because pretty soon people from church show up too.

Just then, Tata and Mama Rosi arrive, and of course, Tata parks his car in front of our house and leaves it running with the radio blasting old music. The two sets of grandparents sit on the chairs my dad brings out onto the grass—they always have a lot to talk about. Then JuJu's dad, my Tío Miguel, shows up with pan dulce from the Mexican bakery and we decide to sell those too.

Señora Sanchez comes over with her grandchildren,

who are visiting, and the whole Washington family stops by. Mr. Martínez even takes a break from his grocery store to come visit. We try to give him a free glass of lemonade, but he insists on paying, so we fill his glass so full that it spills over onto his shoes. I'm going to bring him two cupcakes the next time I make them, I decide.

Some people start dancing and others start arguing over politics and fútbol. The kids yell and play and someone falls and scrapes their knee and someone's mom makes them feel better, and it's a real party.

"¡Fiesta!" yells JuJu.

"It's a party," I agree. "But we're almost out of lemonade!"

"That's only because you said kids six and under drink free," JuJu says.

"I didn't realize how much Javier, Jade, and Lucía could drink." I laugh. I love the twins. We ask Josie to help us sell while we run back in the house to squeeze more lemons until we're sweating and our hands are more than tingling, they're burning. Mama and Tía Sofía come help, and pretty soon we are back in business.

Finally, we close down, because we've run out of sugar, lemons, and energy. Besides, it's getting dark.

Our friends and neighbors leave but our family stays. Dad and Tío Miguel go to a restaurant and pick up chicharrones and Portuguese sweet bread, and we are ready to eat!

But first, JuJu and I bring the money into my bedroom and count it out. We have over a hundred dollars!

"Good profit!" JuJu says.

"Did you bring the real estate lady's number?" I ask.

"Yup, here it is," she says, and pulls a piece of paper out of her pocket. I've borrowed Dad's phone. JuJu gives me the number, and I call.

"Smith Realty, you've reached Molly. How can I help you?" a lady's voice says on the other end.

"Hi, Molly, I'm Sarai Gonzales, and I'm calling for my Tata and my Mama Rosi. They live in the house on Greene Street," I say, trying to sound older than I am.

"Hello, Sarai, how can I help you?" she asks, sounding a little confused.

"I would like to help buy the house," I say, "and I'd like to know how much I will need." There's a long silence at the other end of the phone.

"Are you asking for the sale price of the home?"

"Yes! And how long until we need to have the money?" I ask.

"Well, as your Tata and Mama Rosi know, we already have an offer for the house."

"How much?" I ask. Why won't she tell me?

"Well . . ." she says, and then she says the actual number. No wonder she didn't want to tell me! It's a big number. Way more than we could ever make even if we had time for twenty lemonade stands, which we don't.

"Oh," I say, and I can hardly talk. "Thank you. Bye." I'm shocked.

"Bad news?" JuJu asks.

"Yes," I say with a lump in my throat. "Even if we come in first place at the Garden State Kids Dance-Off, we won't have enough. I don't want you to have to leave."

"Me neither," she says, and we hug each other. "Let's go eat, before everything's gone."

"You go ahead," I say, and sit down on my bed. I look at my "YOU ARE AWESOME" poster, and wonder what I, Sarai, should do now. I can't think of a single awesome answer.

By the time I go to join everyone, they're all inside and the food is almost gone.

"Sarai!" Tata calls. "Come here! I saved you a plate! Barriga llena, corazón contento," Tata says. I eat the delicious food, and then Tía Sofía takes my hand.

"Come dance to this song, Sarai!" It's "Fiesta," by a group called Bomba Estéreo. Their name means stereo bomb, which is what some Colombians use to describe a big party. My parents have pushed back the couch so we have a dance floor, and everyone is on it.

"¡Fiesta! ¡Fiesta! Y ven a bailar y ven a gozar," a voice sings, which means, "Party! Party! Come and dance! Come and enjoy!"

That's exactly what I decide to do. I get up and join the dancing. Tata and Mama Rosi dance and Papá and Mama Chila and the Js and my parents and my sisters and me. JuJu and I show off some of our new Playful Prima moves and everyone claps and pretty soon I'm smiling and laughing and finally I stop thinking and just have fun.

CHAPTER 9

THE SUPER AWESOME
SISTER FUN CLUB

On Sunday morning, Mom and Dad surprise me.

"Sarai," Mom says. "This morning I had a call from Molly Smith, the realtor who is selling Tata and Mama Rosi's house."

Uh-oh. I hope I'm not in trouble.

"You should have talked to us before you called her," Dad says.

"I just wanted to help," I say, "and to surprise everyone."

"We understand that," Mom says, "but next time, come to us first."

"Okay," I say. "I promise. But we can't let someone else buy the house! We have just too many happy memories there, and where will Mama and Tata and the Js go?"

"We'll always have those memories, regardless of whether they live in that house, Sarai," Dad explains.

"Molly did tell us that she was amazed that a little girl would be so committed to helping her grandparents," Mom says, "but she was worried that you seemed upset when you learned the actual cost of the house."

"I was upset," I tell my parents. "But now I'm not, because JuJu and I are going to be famous dancers and we'll make enough money to buy the house. Any day we are going to find out about the audition. I'm not giving up, even if we need to buy the house back from the people who just bought it."

Mom and Dad look at each other, and then at me.

"Sarai," Mom says, "we aren't giving up. You need to learn that sometimes we don't get exactly what we want. We need to be adaptable."

"What does adaptable mean?" I say, frustrated.

"It means we need to be okay with new plans when others fall through. Tata and Mama Rosi will adapt to a new home," Dad explains. "Remember, there isn't only one solution to a problem. And let's look at the positive—maybe Tata and Mama Rosi can find an even better house. Everything will work out. You'll see. Now go get dressed for church."

We go to church together, and amazingly, Josie and Lucía don't get too wiggly during the service. I think they danced so much yesterday, they are too tired to move. It's raining, so we don't go to the park after services, but once we get home, I'm inspired.

I have a super awesome idea. I put all the pillows in my house in one corner of the family room and move an end table there too. Then I collect all the picture books, comic books, magazines, and chapter books I can find and set them up along the wall and on the table. I make a sign that says:

I'm ready to call our first meeting to order. I go into my sisters' room and say, "Josie! Lucía! Come to the family room. I have a surprise."

"Do we have to clean anything?" Josie asks.

"Does it involve typing?" asks Lucía.

"No and no," I say, and sigh. "I know I've been really bossy lately—"

"You have," Lucía agrees.

"Well, I want to make it up to you," I say, "so come into the family room."

The girls can't resist a surprise, so pretty soon they are sitting on pillows in the Reading Corner and looking at me.

"Welcome to the Super Awesome Sister Fun Club!" I tell my sisters. "We are going to meet every Sunday during the school year and even more often during the summer! The first thing I want you to know is that I'm president."

"What are we?" asks Lucía, pointing to herself and Josie. I'm about to tell them that they can be vice presidents, but then I remember why they were mad at me in the first place.

"You are presidents too!" I say. "We are all co-presidents!"

"What are we going to do?" Josie asks.

"Have fun together!" I say. "This week's activity is going to be a relaxing reading session. Next week, Josie will pick what we do, then the week after that, Lucía."

"Dance party!" Josie signs and says.

"Go to Hawaii!" Lucía says.

"That sounds great to me," I say, laughing. I pick up a book, flop down on the pillows, and start to read. My sisters do the same. Mom brings us some hot milk and honey, Dad starts to cook dinner, and I drift into my book.

CHAPTER 10

THE MEANING OF AWESOME

A few weeks later, when Lucía and I walk through the front door after school, we don't see Tata. Instead, we see Mom, Dad, and Josie.

"What's going on?" I ask.

"It's a special day!" Dad says. "I picked up Josie from school early."

"And I took the afternoon off of work," Mom says.

"Why?" Lucía asks. Just then, there is a knock at the door.

AWESOME

family

"I wonder who that is?" Dad says, and opens the door. It's Tata and Mama Rosi and the Js!

"I didn't know you were coming over today!" I say to Mama Rosi.

"We came over to share some great news!" says Tata.

"Great news?" I ask. "What is it?"

"We found a home with Tía Sofía and Tío Miguel! It's big enough for all of us!" Tata explains.

"We are buying it together so it will truly be ours!" Mama Rosi says.

"Does that mean that no one can make you leave?" I ask.

"That's exactly what it means, Sarai!" Tata says.

"Well, when can we see it?" I ask.

"Now!" says JuJu, and gives me a hug.

"Mommy, twelve?" Josie asks and signs. She wants all twelve of us to go together.

"Yes!" Mom says. "All twelve!"

I race to the rectangle and start to get inside, but Tata stops me.

"Sarai, we are going to walk," he says.

"Walk!" Dad says.

"You've got to be kidding me!" Lucía yells. I start hopping up and down.

"You'll be close enough to walk!" I say. "I can't believe it!"

"Believe it," Tata says, and JuJu grabs my hand.

"We are going to have a big dinner tonight to celebrate," Mama Rosi says.

We walk down the street together toward their new home.

"Here comes the Gonzalez family!" Mr. Martínez says as we walk past his store. So of course we have to stop and share our good news.

"¡Felicidades!" he says. "Congratulations!" And off we go.

The house is only a fifteen-minute walk away! Their new house is red. *The exact color of my watermelon cupcakes*, I think, and I know exactly what kind of cupcakes I'm going to make for their housewarming treat.

Tata takes out a key and opens the door, and we all pile in. It's big and sunny.

"Do you like it?" JuJu asks, showing me her room.

"I love it!" I say. "We can walk to each other's houses now!" We hug.

"And Mom says we'll even be at the same school!" JuJu says. "Wait until you see the backyard!"

"Double, triple, quadruple yay!" I say, and I mean it. The Super Awesome Sister Fun Club is going to have to include cousins, I think.

"Are you happy, Sarai?" JuJu asks.

"Yes!" I say. "The happiest ever!"

"Good," she says, "because I need to show you something." She hands me a letter.

Dear Playful Primas:

Thank you for submitting an audition video to this fall's Garden State Kids Dance-Off. We enjoyed watching your video, but unfortunately, you were not selected for the final competition. Keep trying, and remember: You are a rising star!

"Do you know what this means?" I ask JuJu after I read it.

"That we aren't as good as we think we are?" JuJu says.

"No!" I say. "It just means that we need to try harder! The Playful Primas are still going to be famous, maybe just not this week. Agreed?" I ask, raising my hand for a high five.

"Agreed!" JuJu says, high-fiving me. Then we go join the rest of the family to celebrate.

GARDEN STATE   KIDS DANCE-OFF

Dear Playful Primas,

Thank you for submitting an audition video to this fall's Garden State Kids Dance-Off. We enjoyed watching your video, but unfortunately, you were not selected for the final competition. Keep trying, and remember: you are a rising star!

When I get home from Tata and Mama Rosi and the Js' new house, I'm tired but happy. I'm ready to sleep, but there's one more thing I want to do before I go to bed. I look up at the "YOU ARE AWESOME" sign over my bed and I know I need to change it. I take it down, get some construction paper, and make a new one. It says "WE ARE AWESOME!"

I changed it because I am part of the Gonzalez family and we is more fun than just me. I don't always have to be in charge of everything, even if I'd like to be. And even when I am in charge, dreams don't always come true. But sometimes, when family sticks together, they do! And that, I decide, is the real meaning of awesome.